Beware ....
Obedience School
Drop-Out

by GEORGE CRENSHAW

A TOM DOHERTY ASSOCIATES BOOK
NEW YORK

The Cartoons in this volume also appear in the Giant Size BELVEDERE.

This is a work of fiction. All the characters and events portrayed in this book are fictitious, and any resemblance to real people or events is purely coincidental.

BELVEDERE: BEWARE . . . . OBEDIENCE SCHOOL DROP-OUT

A Tor Book
Published by Tom Doherty Associates, Inc.
49 West 24th Street
New York, N.Y. 10010

First printing: May 1991

ISBN: 0-812-51449-1

Printed in the United States of America

0 9 8 7 6 5 4 3 2 1

GEORGE CRENSHAW

 9-3

"NOW THAT YOU MENTION IT, NO-I DON'T SUPPOSE THERE *IS* ANYTHING WRONG WITH A DOG CARRYING HIS BONES IN AN ATTACHE CASE."

8-30

GEORGE CRENSHAW

"ALL RIGHT. WHAT HAVE YOU DONE ***NOW*** ?!"

BEWARE OF
LOW FLYING
AIRCRAFT

8-29

GEORGE
CRENSHAW

GEORGE
CRENSHAW

9-1

"DID THAT LETTER ABOUT MY FAMILY TREE COME YET?"

"DON'T BE RIDICULOUS. THAT'S THE DOG'S NATURAL EXPRESSION. HE DIDN'T GET THAT WAY CHASING PARKED CARS."

NO PEOPLE ALLOWED

GEORGE CRENSHAW

7-26

"WHO CARES HOW HE DOES IT, AS LONG AS HE GETS THE JOB DONE!"

"THEY'VE FORMED A CONDOMINIUM."

GEORGE CRENSHAW 7-25

"LOOK AT IT THIS WAY. FOR A DOG YOU'RE LUCKY TO JUST HAVE A T.V. SET. MAYBE NEXT YEAR YOU CAN HAVE COLOR."

GEORGE CRENSHAW

FUN, TRICKS & STUNTS

7-19

"OK, I'M HOLDING THE GLASS FULL OF WATER TIGHT AGAINST THE CEILING WITH THE BROOM. NOW WHAT'S THE REST OF THE TRICK?"

GEORGE CRENSHAW

7-22

"THERE'S SUCH A THING AS A *NUT-CRACKER*, YOU KNOW!"

5-19

GEORGE CRENSHAW

I HAVEN'T THE HEART TO TELL HIM WE'VE DRAINED THE POOL."

"THEY'VE ADDED TWO NEW DOG-CATCHERS WHO LOOK ALIKE, AND BOTH NAMED *ED*."

"WELL, TWO *ED'S* ARE BETTER THAN ONE!"

GEORGE CRENSHAW

7-18

"KEEP YOUR EARS OPEN. THE MONARCH MOOSE CAN SOMETIMES BE VERY SNEAKY!"

"IF YOU HAVEN'T, THEN TELL ME - JUST **WHO** ELSE AROUND HERE WOULD BE SMOKING MY CIGARS?"

7-15 GEORGE CRENSHAW © FIELD ENTERPRISES, INC., 1977

"MAYBE WE OUGHTA BREAK DOWN AND TAKE HIM ON A HOUSE BOAT VACATION."

"-AND WAY UP THERE IS LOVER'S LEAP."

"HE'S NOT A BACK ALLEY FIGHTER LIKE JUST *ANY* ORDINARY DOG."

AL'S SLIM GYM

GEORGE CRENSHAW

9-2

"SEE IF YOU CAN QUALIFY FOR A GROUP RATE."

GEORGE CRENSHAW

5-21

"HEY! WHEN I SAID *KILL THE LIGHT* I MEANT . . . ."

"ALL RIGHT. WHO'S BEEN SMOKING MY CIGARS?"

"I WON'T EXACTLY SAY HE'S A LOUSY COOK, BUT HE'S THE ONLY CHEF IN THE WORLD WHO CAN BURN A SALAD!"

GEORGE CRENSHAW

6-3

"IT WAS THE ONLY WAY WE COULD GET HIM TO SLEEP IN THE BASEMENT."

GEORGE CRENSHAW

FLEA MARKET

5-30

GEORGE CRENSHAW

6-4

"I TOLD HIM TO WATER THE BACK YARD. NOW WOULDN'T YOU KNOW HE'D FIGURE AN *EASY* WAY OUT?!"

GEORGE CRENSHAW

5-26

"DON'T BE A WISE GUY. MY BROTHER RALPH IS HOME IN ALTOONA, AND YOU KNOW IT."

"YOU'VE GOT TO ADMIT- HIS INTENTIONS ARE HONORABLE."

CITY WATER DEPT.

GEORGE CRENSHAW

6-9

"WHAT WILL HE THINK OF NEXT?"

GEORGE CRENSHAW

© FIELD ENTERPRISES, INC., 1977

6-10

"OVER 50 DOGS ON THE BLOCK AND HE HAD TO FALL FOR A WATER SPANIEL."

"YOU DON'T SEE MANY DOG HOUSES THESE DAYS WITH A JACUZZI."

6-6

GEORGE CRENSHAW

"YEAH! HOW DID YOU KNOW MT. ARARAT IS JUST UP AHEAD?"

GEORGE CRENSHAW

6-18

"I CAN ALWAYS TELL WHEN HE'S PEEVED ABOUT SOMETHING."

GEORGE CRENSHAW

6-15

"AT LAST WE'VE DISCOVERED THE SOURCE OF THE AMAZON!"

GEORGE CRENSHAW

6-21

"NO, YOU CANNOT HAVE $795.63!"

"OH STOP WORRYING ABOUT BEARS, COUGARS, SNAKES AND BIGFOOT. WE'RE WILD AND WOOLY MOUNTAINEERS, REMEMBER ?"

"OH, ALL RIGHT. YOU CAN MASH THE POTATOES IF YOU INSIST."

"YOU JUST SAW THE WORLD'S FIRST HOLE-IN-ZERO. HE MISSED THE BALL AND SANK THE DIVOT!"

7-1

GEORGE CRENSHAW

"YOU AND YOUR SHORT CUTS!"

GEORGE CRENSHAW

6-30

"HOLD IT!"

GEORGE CRENSHAW

7-21

"ARF! ARF!"

"ALL RIGHT. WHO FIXED THE T.V.?"

GEORGE CRENSHAW 6-28

"CAN'T YOU TELL AN OLD RUSSIAN ROULETTE PLAYER WHEN YOU SEE ONE?"

6-27

GEORGE CRENSHAW

"NO, YOU MAY NOT CAN THEM!"

7-23

GEORGE CRENSHAW

"SO ORV SAID, WHY SEND HIM TO OBEDIENCE SCHOOL? I'LL TEACH HIM MYSELF."

"NO, IT'S NOT AN OBEDIENCE SCHOOL DIPLOMA. IT'S AN AWARD FROM CITY SANITATION FOR NOT TIPPING OVER A TRASH PAIL FOR THREE WHOLE SUCCESSIVE DAYS."

7-8

GEORGE CRENSHAW

"IT WAS RIGHT HERE WHERE WE WINGED ONE LAST YEAR."

6-20

GEORGE CRENSHAW

"NOW DON'T BE ANGRY, DEAR. BELVEDERE WAS JUST TRYING TO HELP WITH THE GARDENING."

"WOULD YOU MIND WHISTLING SOME OTHER TUNE?"

GEORGE CRENSHAW

CHOW

6-14

"WE SHOULD NEVER HAVE GIVEN HIM THAT BOOK ON LEVITATION!"

GEORGE CRENSHAW

7-5

"WOULD THERE BE ANY MESSAGE?"

GEORGE CRENSHAW

7-4

"ALL RIGHT. I BELIEVE YOU. MAYBE THOSE WERE *BIGFOOT* TRACKS WE SAW."

"HE INSISTED ON SOME KIND OF A STATUS SYMBOL."

"I LOVE THIS PLACE, I BROUGHT BELVEDERE HERE LAST YEAR AND HE GOT LOST FOR THREE WEEKS."

"WILL YOU BE MUCH LONGER WATCHING YOUR CARTOONS, ORVILLE? BELVEDERE WANTS TO WATCH THE PRESIDENT'S ADDRESS."

"GOT HIM!"

GEORGE CRENSHAW

8-15

"I ACCIDENTALLY SAID **SYRINGE**."

GEORGE CRENSHAW

8-13

"WHY DOES THERE ALWAYS HAVE TO BE ONE CLOWN IN EVERY HOUSEHOLD?"

GEORGE CRENSHAW

8-17

"SO WHAT IF I AM SITTING ON YOUR FAVORITE CHAIR. WHAT ARE YOU GOING TO DO ABOUT IT ?"

8-23

GEORGE CRENSHAW

"HE ENTERTAINS A LOT."

8-26

GEORGE CRENSHAW

"I STILL SAY WE'RE SPOILING HIM."

POLICE

8-3

GEORGE CRENSHAW

"KNOCK IT OFF!... THE POLICE HAVE ENOUGH PROBLEMS WITHOUT YOUR IMITATION OF EDWARD G. ROBINSON!"

"HE'S STARTING A *HAREM!*"

"DON'T LAUGH, DEAR. IT WILL ONLY ENCOURAGE HIM."

"WELL, WHO WON THE BIG GAME?"

"HOW'S DADDY'S LITTLE HELPER?"

VETERINARIAN

X-RAY

8-22 GEORGE CRENSHAW

"NO, IT IS NOT SOMETHING HE SWALLOWED. THAT, SIR, IS THE CANINE STOMACH."

GEORGE CRENSHAW

8-2

"HE'S JUST FULL OF DOGGIE TRICKS TODAY."

"WHY CAN'T HE HAVE JUST AN ORDINARY SIZE PET ROCK?"

"YOU'LL NEVER CATCH ANYTHING WITH THOSE MECHANICAL FISHING LURES."

"I STILL SAY YOU'RE SPOILING THEM!"

"FORGET IT. IT'LL NEVER WORK."

"HE SWIMS 22 LAPS IN LESS THAN AN HOUR. OF COURSE, HE CAN GO FASTER WHEN THE POOL'S FILLED WITH WATER."

GEORGE CRENSHAW

12-31

"HE'S NOT BEGGING FOR BONES.. HE WANTS A CUP OF GIN."

"NO NIPPING AT MAILMEN. NO NIPPING AT MAILMEN. TIPPING GARBAGE PAILS IS A NO-NO. TIPPING GARBAGE PAILS IS A NO-NO. I'LL NOT BARK AT CARS..."

5-13

GEORGE CRENSHAW

"I WONDERED WHY HE BROUGHT ALONG THAT SAW."

Sam's BUTCHER SHOP

8-12

GEORGE CRENSHAW

"MAYBE WE SHOULD HAVE GOTTEN HIM THE PORTERHOUSE INSTEAD OF HORSEMEAT."

GEORGE CRENSHAW

8-16

"NOW GET RIGHT DOWN FROM THERE AND TELL THE NICE MAN YOU'RE SORRY."

5-12 GEORGE CRENSHAW

"WHY DID WE EVER LET HIM TAKE UP KARATE ?"

"BELVEDERE JUST LOVES TO DEMONSTRATE OUR NEW ROLLAWAY."

"OH, DEAR! IT'S ONE MINUTE PAST HIS FEEDING TIME."

"YOU DIDN'T EXPECT HIM TO *RUN* AWAY FROM HOME LIKE AN ORDINARY DOG, DID YOU?"

"NO, NO, I TOLD YOU WE DON'T BUILD THE WINDOW FIRST."

BEWARE OF
OBEDIENCE
SCHOOL
DROPOUT

JIFFY
SALES

NAT

2-2

DEATH
VALLEY

GEORGE
CRENSHAW

2-3

"HERE WE ARE – 276 FEET BELOW SEA LEVEL.
WHO WOULD EVER BELIEVE IT ?!"

GEORGE CRENSHAW

12-22

"NOW THAT'S WHAT I CALL A WATCHDOG!"

GEORGE CRENSHAW

12-23

"PUTTING MY BEAR TRAP IN THAT OLD BEE HIVE... NOW JUST WHAT DID YOU EXPECT TO CATCH?"

"BUT I STILL DON'T UNDERSTAND WHY YOU WANT ME RIGHT UNDER THIS SIGN?!"

GEORGE CRENSHAW

1-12

"HE GETS HIS WHOLE DAY'S QUOTA WITH ONE CHASE."

GEORGE CRENSHAW

1-13

"DEAR, YOU REMEMBER MR. SPLEEN, OUR BUTCHER!"

GEORGE CRENSHAW

12-24

"SO WE DON'T HAVE A CHIMNEY. SANTA SOMETIMES COMES THROUGH THE DOOR, YOU KNOW!"

GEORGE CRENSHAW

1-19

"DON'T BE RIDICULOUS. WE'RE NOT ANYWHERE NEAR THE SOUTH POLE."

GEORGE CRENSHAW

12-27

"ORVILLE, I CAN'T FIND MY TEETH."

"HOW'S THAT FOR FANCY FETCHING?"

"HE WAS READY FOR A 1-2. IT WAS THE 3-4-5-6 THAT GOT HIM."

"BE QUIET. HE'LL WANT TO GO IF HE HEARS US."

"OH, GOOD GRIEF. I SHOULD NEVER HAVE EVEN MENTIONED IT'S A DOGWOOD TREE."

"THAT'S NOT HOW WE DRESS THE TURKEY!"

"AND WHAT, MAY I ASK, WAS WRONG WITH THE OLD SIGN?"

GEORGE CRENSHAW

12-29

"I'VE NEVER SEEN HIM BEFORE EITHER."

"NOW THAT'S WHAT I CALL A CLASSIC FIGURE EIGHT."

GEORGE CRENSHAW

2-15

"Y'KNOW HE'S RIGHT. IF YOU HAVE ***DOGFISH*** AND ***DOGTREES*** WHY DON'T YOU HAVE ***PEOPLEFISH*** AND ***PEOPLETREES?***"

2-14

GEORGE CRENSHAW

"HE MADE IT ESPECIALLY FOR YOU, DEAR - A CLOCK FOR PEOPLE WHO NEVER TAKE A DRINK BEFORE FIVE O'CLOCK."

12-15

GEORGE CRENSHAW

GEORGE CRENSHAW

12-25

"MY VIOLINS? SNOWSHOES? YOU'VE GOT TO BE KIDDING."

GEORGE CRENSHAW

4-28

"YES, I DID ASK BELVEDERE TO DEFROST THE REFRIGERATOR. WHY?"

GEORGE CRENSHAW

12-16

"DON'T TELL ME, LET ME GUESS. YOU TORE UP THE NEIGHBOR'S YARD... YOU BIT THE MAILMAN AGAIN... YOU CHEWED UP MY NEW SLIPPERS..."

VETERINARIAN

DR. BARKAM

GEORGE CRENSHAW

4-30

"TRY TO RELAX."

"ISN'T THIS RATHER RIDICULOUS FOR A RABBIT HUNT?"

"REMEMBER THE GOOD OLD DAYS WHEN HE USED TO JUST BARK AT PASSERS-BY?"

GEORGE CRENSHAW

4-25

"WE'RE ON THE PATH OF A VERY TRICKY BEAR!"

KENNELWOOD OBEDIENCE SCHOOL

4-21

GEORGE CRENSHAW

"YOU'RE RIGHT, THAT *IS* BELVEDERE'S TRAINER!"

4-19 GEORGE CRENSHAW

"WHY COULDN'T YOU JUST ASK FOR A DOGGIE BAG?"

4-20 GEORGE CRENSHAW

"AWRIGHT! WHO ATE MY FROG'S LEGS?"

4-18

GEORGE RENSHAW

"I SHOULD HAVE KNOWN BETTER THAN TO ASK YOU TO APPLY A LITTLE FIRST AID."

GEORGE RENSHAW

1-7

1-4

"ACTUALLY THE WIND BLEW IT OVER, BUT HE'S MAKING THE MOST OF IT."

1-7

"HE SAYS IF HE JUST SELLS ONE GLASS HE'S GOT IT MADE FOR THE MONTH."

"HE HATES TO BE PUT OUT FOR THE NIGHT."

"THERE'S GOT TO BE AN EASIER WAY TO KILL A FLY."

GEORGE CRENSHAW

5-9

"ADMIT IT OLD BUDDY, YOU'RE MAD AT ME ABOUT SOMETHING, AREN'T YOU?"

GEORGE CRENSHAW

5-7

"NOW THAT'S WHAT I CALL A WATCH DOG!"

"CITY TRASH COLLECTORS. BELVEDERE'S BEEN AT IT AGAIN."

"YOU NAME IT- BELVEDERE AND I HAVE CHASED IT."

1-6

GEORGE CRENSHAW

"DON'T ASK HIM TO CUT THE CARDS."

1-5

GEORGE CRENSHAW

"HERE HE COMES WITH ANOTHER ONE OF HIS FISH STORIES."

"THIS IS THE HUMOROUS VERSION OF THEIR TRIP INTO HEAD-HUNTER TERRITORY."

"YOU DON'T SEE MANY DOGHOUSES WITH A WINE CELLAR."

TREE S

Z. FUTTS
TREE
SURGEON

GEORGE CRENSHAW

2-19

© FIELD ENTERPRISES, INC., 1977

"OKAY, YOUR OPINION IS *TIRED SAP*. NOW CAN WE GET ANOTHER OPINION?"

"ALL RIGHT! ALL RIGHT! YOU'RE GONNA GET FED!"

GEORGE CRENSHAW

2-18

"WHADDYA MEAN, YOU'RE MAKING MILK-SHAKES FOR THE GANG!!?"

GEORGE CRENSHAW

5-3

"IT'S HIS ONLY OUTLET, SINCE THE NEIGHBORS MADE HIM QUIT CHASING CARS."

GEORGE CRENSHAW

1-3

"SURE THERE'S NOT ***SOMETHING*** YOU FORGOT THIS MORNING?"

GEORGE CRENSHAW

1-26

"IT'S ONLY A HUNCH, BUT I'VE GOT A FUNNY FEELING IT'S GOING TO BE ONE OF THOSE UNLUCKY DAYS."

GEORGE CRENSHAW

3-18

"YES, DEAR, IT HAS BEEN A LITTLE EXTRA LOAD TO PACK, BUT YOU KNOW HOW HE COMPLAINS ABOUT SLEEPING ON THE HARD GROUND."

ALL DOGS MUST BE ON LEASH

GEORGE CRENSHAW

3-23

"I WONDERED WHY HE WANTED TO BUY A WIND-UP TOY."

"SO YOU THINK YOU'VE INVENTED A TIME MACHINE?" HOW ABSOLUTELY RIDICULOUS!"

"OH, ALL RIGHT. ALL RIGHT. SO IT'S LOW TIDE."

GEORGE CRENSHAW

3-10

GEORGE CRENSHAW

3-11

"FRANKLY, I DON'T THINK HE'S AN OFFICIAL-NEIGHBORHOOD-STEAK-AND-LOBSTER-TESTER AT ALL!"

"NOW JUST ONE MINUTE!"

"WATCH OUT FOR HIS OVERHEAD SMASH."

GEORGE CRENSHAW

3-10

"THEY MADE A PACT. ORVILLE'S QUITTING SMOKING IF BELVEDERE QUITS GARBAGE PAILS."

GEORGE CRENSHAW

4-2

GEORGE CRENSHAW

9-8

"NO DOUBT ABOUT IT, OLD PAL - THE WHITE SPOTTED PUP HAS ***GOTTA*** BE YOURS."

GEORGE CRENSHAW

3-28

"OH, DON'T GET SO UPSET ABOUT IT. MAYBE NEXT YEAR THEY'LL HAVE A BIONIC DOG SHOW."

"OH, WHAT IS IT NOW."

GEORGE CRENSHAW

3-5

"AND DURING THE OLD TARZAN MOVIES, HE ROOTS FOR THE CROCODILES."

GEORGE CRENSHAW

4-4

"THIS IS THE SPOT I WAS TELLING YOU ABOUT."

GEORGE CRENSHAW

3-21

"WELL, SPEAK UP! DID YOU OR DIDN'T YOU LOCK BELVEDERE IN THE BASEMENT FOR THE NIGHT?"

GEORGE CRENSHAW

3-30

"HOW GOES THE BATTLE, FELLAS?"

GEORGE CRENSHAW

3-31

"BELVEDERE ALWAYS LIKES TO PLAY WITH HIS PREY BEFORE THE KILL."

GEORGE CRENSHAW

3-29

"SO YOU GOT A NIBBLE. BIG DEAL."

GEORGE CRENSHAW

4-5

"HE'S JUST FULL OF DOGGIE TRICKS TODAY!"

GEORGE CRENSHAW

4-6

"THEY'RE ALWAYS THIS WAY FOR AWHILE AFTER A LONG DUCK HUNT."

GEORGE CRENSHAW

3-22

"I THINK HE'S GOT SOMETHING THERE. HE'S INVENTED A TWO-WAY SHOE FOR PEOPLE WHO DON'T KNOW WHETHER THEY'RE COMING OR GOING."

GEORGE CRENSHAW

1-28

"SOMEONE'S GOTTEN INTO OUR SUPPLIES."

"SO WHAT'S SO GREAT ABOUT SIX MILLION DOLLAR MAN? WE'VE GOT A POOCH WITH BIONIC TASTE BUDS!"

"WE'RE SELDOM BOTHERED WITH PEDDLERS."

"*NOW* WILL YOU ADMIT WE'RE LOST?"

"I'LL NOT BE NEEDING A SEAT BELT, THANK YOU."

"BELVEDERE ALWAYS SEEMS TO KNOW WHEN YOU'RE HEADING OUT ON YOUR NIGHT-ON-THE-TOWN WITH THE FELLAS!"

"KEEP YOUR EYES AND EARS OPEN, MEN. HE'S HERE IN THE NEIGHBORHOOD SOMEWHERE."

"GOOD BOY. I NEEDED A BOARD JUST THAT SIZE."

GEORGE CRENSHAW

2-28

"WHEN YOU INSISTED ON AN ASTRO-TURF YARD, HE HAD TO BURY HIS BONES *SOMEHOW*."

GEORGE CRENSHAW

4-15

"I TOLD YOU NOT TO LET HIM NEAR THE NEW WATER BED!"

"HE ACCIDENTALLY HEARD YOU OPEN THE REFRIGERATOR DOOR."

"ATTACH A GENERATOR TO HIS MOUTH, AND WE'D HAVE THE ANSWER TO THE ENERGY SHORTAGE!"

"IT WAS CUTE AT FIRST. NOW HE'S GOT THE HABIT."

GEORGE CRENSHAW

4-26

"GOOD HEAVENS, DON'T LOAN HIM YOUR GUN. DO YOU WANT TO UPSET THE WORLD BALANCE OF POWER?!"

BELVEDERE

7-30

GEORGE CRENSHAW

GEORGE CRENSHAW

8-6

"OK, SO WE GOT LOST ON A FARM, AND I WASN'T WEARING MY GLASSES THAT DAY. NOW TAKE THAT DOWN!"

GEORGE CRENSHAW

2-12

GEORGE CRENSHAW

2-9

"THAT'S RIGHT. I TOLD BELVEDERE HE COULD HAVE JUST ONE PIECE OF CHICKEN BEFORE DINNER."

4-16

GEORGE CRENSHAW

GEORGE CRENSHAW

1-2

"REMEMBER THE GOOD OLD DAYS WHEN HE WAS SATISFIED WITH JUST A RUBBER DOGGIE BONE AND A SQUEAK MOUSE?"

GEORGE CRENSHAW

8-1

"WHATEVER YOU DO, DON'T GET HIM STARTED ON THE SUBJECT OF ECOLOGY."

"WHY CAN'T HE JUST CHASE CARS AND CATS LIKE OTHER DOGS?"

"OKAY, SO WHERE'S THE FRISBEE?"

8-4 NAT

"YOU'VE GONE ONE STEP TOO FAR WITH YOUR BIRD-DOG TRAINING"

9-6 NAT

" I THINK WE'D BETTER LET HIM IN SOON. "

CITY POUND

127

 7-27

GEORGE CRENSHAW

"LET'S GO, PIEDGRASS—WE'LL GET THE BEST OF **HIM** TODAY."

NAT 4-7

"SO YOU'VE BEEN HEARING A DRIPPY-DRIP-DRIP. GO BACK TO BED."

NAT 8-10

"I THINK IT'S A SIDE-WINDER!"

NAT 7-8

"IF HE COULD ONLY SWIM."

"YOU'RE PUSHING YOUR LUCK AGAIN!"

"HE HAS A REAL TALENT FOR CEILINGS."

GEORGE CRENSHAW

8-7

"I'M GOING SHOPPING AND I WANT TO SEE TWO FISH IN THAT BOWL WHEN I GET BACK."

NAT

6-2

" THEY MAKE A GREAT TEAM. "

NAT 8-13

"BELVEDERE WARMED UP YOUR SHAVING BOMB ON THE BATHROOM HEATER. HOW THOUGHTFUL OF HIM."

NAT 8-14

"ORVILLE, BELVEDERE IS WAITING FOR YOU TO TAKE HIM ROMPING."

GEORGE CRENSHAW

INCOME TAX

7-18

"ABOUT THIS DEDUCTION FOR CHEWED UP SHOES AND TORN UP GARDENS ?..."

8-16

NAT

"LET'S GIVE UP THE SEARCH. ALL THOSE STORIES ABOUT BIGFOOT ARE A LOT OF HOGWASH ANYWAY."

GEORGE CRENSHAW 7-30

"DID YOU HAVE TO TELL CHI CHI THE BIRD-WATCHERS WERE IN TOWN?"

"I SENT HIM AFTER A PINT OF ICE CREAM, WHY?"

GEORGE CRENSHAW

10-31

"CHI CHI'S ON OUR ELECTRIC BLANKET AGAIN. HMM, I THINK THAT EXPLAINS THOSE HARD-BOILED EGGS SHE'S BEEN LAYING."

7-14

NAT

" ALL RIGHT, WHO FILLED THIS THERMOS ? "

BAZ

GEORGE CRENSHAW 6-23

"DON'T HEDGE ANY LONGER. YOU KNOW YOU PROMISED TO PLAY BALL WITH HIM."

"IF YOU DON'T LIKE THE TUNE, JUST SAY SO!"

TELEPHONE

6-5

" OH, WHY DON'T WE LET HIM MAKE JUST ONE PHONE CALL TO HIS LAWYER IF HE INSISTS. "

6-6

" ELECTION BET OR NOT, I STILL SAY IT'S A VIOLATION OF THE CITY LEASH ORDINANCE ! "

6-4

NAT

"REMEMBER THE GOOD OLD DAYS WHEN HE USED TO JUST ROMP AROUND THE PARK?"

NAT

6-16

"HE SELDOM GETS CAUGHT."

NAT 6-27

"ISN'T THAT NICE OF BELVEDERE OFFERING TO DEFROST THE REFRIGERATOR FOR ME?"

7-16

NAT

" THERE'S GOT TO BE AN EASIER WAY TO PULL A TOOTH ! "

"I DON'T KNOW, BUT IT MUST HAVE SOMETHING TO DO WITH HIS FEUD WITH THE DOG CATCHER."

"HE INSISTED."

7-18 NAT

" NOW WAS THAT A NICE THING TO DO TO MY FLAPJACKS ? "

NAT 7-19

" WHY CAN'T HE JUST EAT GRASS WHEN HE'S SICK ? "

NAT 7-7

"DOES HE HAVE TO MAKE A GAME OUT OF *EVERYTHING*?!"

7-8

NAT

"HE ALWAYS THINKS OF SOMETHING WHEN I RUN OUT OF AMMUNITION."

7-9

NAT

" WHEN I SAID 'GET THE PHONE,' I MEANT ANSWER IT. "

NAT

7-10

" BARKING AT PARKED CAR WHEELS ?... NOW IF THAT ISN'T THE HEIGHT OF LAZINESS! "

NAT

7-11

" HE LOVES A GOOD KANGAROO HUNT. "

9 FT.

NAT 7-12

"BELVEDERE ALWAYS GIVES ORVILLE A SLIGHT HANDICAP WHEN THEY RACE."

"GOOD GRIEF-IF HE WANTED TO BAKE SOMETHING, WHY DID YOU LET HIM READ YOUR PRETZEL RECIPE?"

"I'LL BE DANGED! LITTLE JOE, THE HARD WAY!"

7-23

" OH, DEAR -- I THINK YOU QUITE POSSIBLY DO HAVE WATER ON THE BRAIN. "

7-24

" DOES HE ALWAYS HAVE TO ANALYZE EVERY MEAL I PUT OUT ? "

NAT 7-25

"ADMIT IT, ORVILLE. YOU HAVE FINALLY MET UP WITH A SUPERIOR ADVERSARY."

CONSTRUCTION UNDERWAY
AJAX PIPE

NAT

7-29

"ON THE OTHER HAND, IT COULD BE TWO DOGS!"

NAT

7-28

" WHAT HAVE YOU DONE TO HELP? AT LEAST GIVE HIM CREDIT FOR TRYING. "

7-31

NAT

" ADMIT IT. YOU'RE MAD ABOUT SOMETHING, AREN'T YOU? "

"TAKE IT EASY. THEY NEVER PRINTED ONE OF MY LETTERS TO THE EDITOR EITHER."

"WE SHOULD NEVER HAVE ASKED HIM TO HELP."

NAT 7-30

"OH, GOOD GRIEF. HAVEN'T YOU EVER HEARD AN ELEPHANT TRUMPET BEFORE?"

1

SCORE

6-25

NAT

"OH, COME NOW! I'M NOT *THAT* LOUSY AND YOU KNOW IT!"

EEEEE-YAH!

6-26

NAT

" WHY DID YOU EVER ASK HIM TO SLICE THE SALAMI ? "

NAT

6-30

" WELL, AT LEAST IT'S BETTER THAN THE FROWZY POODLE HE BROUGHT HOME LAST SATURDAY NIGHT ! "

"WELL, YOU **DID** ASK HIM TO GET YOU A HAMBURGER, WITH **EVERYTHING** ON IT."

"HE WON'T COME FOR JUST ANY ORDINARY WHISTLE."

"IT'S THE SAME THING AT HOME. HE WON'T LISTEN TO ANYTHING BUT STEREO."

" YOU FIXED THAT LEAKY HOSE NOZZLE? GOOD BOY! "

7-3

" STOP COMPLAINING. AT LEAST YOU GOT A BITE. "

7-4

" SO I'M LEAVING FOR WORK AN HOUR EARLIER THIS MORNING. NOW WHAT'S SO FUNNY ? "

"IT WAS **SUPPOSED** TO BE FLAMING!"

" I GIVE UP. WHAT **DID** YOU PAINT WHILE I WAS ASLEEP? "

8-11

NAT

"CAREFUL WHERE YOU SHOOT. I'VE HEARD THERE ARE SOMETIMES CHILDREN PLAYING IN THESE WOODS."

NAT

6-18

"WHY CAN'T HE JUST BURY HIS BONES IN THE BACK YARD?"

8-2

NAT

"HE'S WAITING FOR THE MAILMAN. TODAY HE GRADUATES FROM HIS OBEDIENCE CORRESPONDENCE COURSE."

NAT

6-19

"I SAID THEY'RE BRINGING IT BACK TOMORROW!"

NAT

3-26

"WHY CAN'T HE JUST CHASE **CARS** LIKE OTHER DOGS DO?"

NAT

3-27

"WELL, THAT'S ONE MORE BURGLAR WE DON'T HAVE TO WORRY ABOUT."

"I'M SORRY I ASKED HIM WHAT THE BOOK WAS ABOUT."